Zero to Hero

Seb Goffe

A & C Black • London

First published 2012 by A & C Black,
an imprint of Bloomsbury Publishing Plc
50 Bedford Square, London WC1B 3DP

www.acblack.com

Copyright © 2012 Seb Goffe
Illustrations copyright © 2012 Bob Moulder

The rights of Seb Goffe and Bob Moulder to be identified
as the author and illustrator of this work have been asserted by them
in accordance with the Copyrights, Designs and Patents Act 1988.

ISBN 978-1-4081-5560-8

A CIP catalogue for this book is available from the British Library.

This book is produced using paper that is made from wood
grown in managed, sustainable forests. It is natural, renewable
and recyclable. The logging and manufacturing processes conform
to the environmental regulations of the country of origin.

Printed by CPI Group (UK), Croydon, CR0 4YY

recommended by

www.catchup.org

Catch Up is a not-for-profit charity
which aims to address the problem of
underachievement that has its roots in
literacy and numeracy difficulties.

ZERO TO HERO

For my nephew, Will

Contents

Chapter One

Throwing It Away

"Come on, Ravens!" shouted Will. "Just hold onto the ball!"

Ravenshill were leading by one goal to nil but the other team were fighting back.

Will and his best friend, Steve were on the touchline and cheering on the Ravens. "They will never hold on to the lead," said Will. "Not playing like this."

Steve nodded, and huddled into his coat. The rain was freezing cold. Steve didn't know why Will watched every game the school team played. After all, Will hadn't been picked for a team since junior school. But he was always there on the touch line.

The ball flew into the Ravenshill penalty area. The keeper punched it out, but only as far as the edge of the box.

A player from the other team got to the ball and fired a low hard shot at goal that ended up in the corner of the net.

A ragged cheer came up from the away fans. The ref blew a long blast on his whistle, and the game was over. The draw meant that Ravenshill were now very close to being relegated from their league.

"Come on," said Steve. "I'm soaked, I want to get home."

Will looked over at the Ravens team, who were listening to their coach, Mr Smith. He was sure Mr Smith would be telling them that the other team wanted to win more than they did.

"That's the third game in a row we've messed up, even though we were in the lead," said Will as he and Steve made their way home.

"We can't spend a whole match chasing the ball," he went on. "We need to bring our midfield in to control the game more. We can't just rely on being stronger and quicker than the other team."

"I suppose you think you know it all," said Steve. "Just because you can't get in the team because you're so small!" He knew this was mean, but he was fed up and very cold. "I suppose you think you'd make a difference to the team?"

"I might," said Will, "if I was ever given a chance. But if Smithy wants to fill his team with sprinters and giants, what can I do?"

Every year Will tried out for the team but he never got picked. He just couldn't compete with players like Adam, the team's star striker.

"I don't know," said Steve. "Maybe Smithy's tactics *are* useless, but he's still the coach."

They had reached the end of Steve's road. "See you at school," he said, and Will walked the rest of the way home on his own.

Chapter Two

Practice Makes Perfect

"Did they win?" Will's mum asked as he got home.

"No," he replied. "We threw it away again. I'm going outside to practise a bit."

"But it's tipping it down out there, you'll get soaked!" said his mum.

"I'm already soaked, Mum!" shouted Will. He went out into the garden, and fished his football out from under a bush.

Will was completely football mad, and practised every single day. Sometimes he'd practise with Steve in the park. But some days when Steve was in a mood or couldn't be bothered, Will practised on his own.

He flicked the ball into the air and started doing keepy-uppies. Right foot, left foot, right foot... one, two, three...

When he got to ten he trapped the ball under his left foot, took a step back and kicked it towards the wall. He was aiming for a small circle painted half-way up.

The wet ball thudded into the wall just below the circle, and rolled back towards Will.

Good, but not perfect, thought Will. He knew if he was ever going to get a chance in the team, he had to be the best to make up for his small size.

He started the routine again but using his right foot for the final kick. This time he hit the circle bang in the middle.

He kept this up for a while, aiming at different marks on the wall from different distances using both feet.

Then he dribbled around his set of training cones. At the end of each run he bounced the ball off the wall, controlled it, and started again.

His mum called him in for supper, but
before he went in to eat he had one last go at
keepy-uppies, just to see how many he could
do.

He almost got to fifty, but skewed the ball off his left foot and lost it. He chased after the loose ball, and hammered it towards the wall, just hitting the edge of the circle.

He smiled, and then headed in before his mum got tired of waiting. When his chance in the team came, he knew he'd be ready.

Chapter Three

In With a Chance?

The next Monday, as Will walked through the school gates, the playground seemed a lot less noisy than usual.

"Hey Steve!" he said. "Where is everyone today?"

"There's a flu bug going round," said Steve. "Some of the football team have got it. Mr Smith is holding trials to get a team out for this weekend's match. There's a notice up in the main hall."

Will's mind raced. Maybe this would be his big chance. If he could get in the team for one game, he could play so well they would have to keep him in the side, even after everyone had got better from the flu.

"How many players are away?" he asked Steve.

"Four or five," said Steve. "So they can't just make do with the usual subs."

"Cool," said Will. "I'm going to go and sign up. See you in English."

Will hurried off to the hall to find the notice. He saw Steve's name and a few others on the list. He hoped there wouldn't be so many others he'd miss out again.

Mr Smith had called a practice that afternoon. Will texted his mum to let her know he'd be home late, and put his name on the list.

Chapter Four

The Trial

"Right," said Mr Smith when all the boys had arrived. "We need to put out a team against Kingham on Saturday or we forfeit the match. Now, even using our subs there are still three gaps in the team: left wing, centre back and right back."

Will's heart sank. There was no chance of him getting the place on the wing, or in central defence, because he wasn't fast or tall enough.

What he'd been hoping for was a chance in midfield, where he could show off his passing and ball control, but it looked like the only chance he would get would be at right back.

"James and Ed, you're the tallest," said Mr Smith, "so you can try out for centre back. I need someone quick on the wing. David and Joe, you can take it in turns to play there." Mr Smith looked over at Will and Steve. "That leaves you two to try out for right back."

Will and Steve looked at each other. They would be going head to head for one place in the team, so one of them would have to miss out.

"Good luck, I suppose," said Steve as Will got ready for the start of the trial. He was facing David on the wing, who was pretty good.

Mr Smith blew his whistle.

Will had never played in defence before, and even playing in the park with Steve, tackling had never been one of his strong points. He did his best to keep track of David. But the winger was just too quick, and time after time Will lost out.

The forwards on David's side kept sending the ball to him as they knew he could out-run Will.

After a bit, Mr Smith asked Steve to swap places with Will.

Steve was up against Joe, another very
quick player. But Steve was faster than Will
was, and he got in a couple of good tackles.

Will could see Mr Smith nodding as he watched the game. He knew his chances of getting into the team were fading fast.

When Mr Smith announced who was in at the end of the match, Will did his best to look pleased for his friend, but all he could think of was that he would be spending another game standing on the sidelines.

Chapter Five

One Man Down

Match day arrived. Will knew the Ravens would probably lose. He was going to cheer on his best mate but really he wanted to be out on the pitch.

Mr Smith was talking to the team, and Will could see Steve and the other new players being given extra advice. Then Mr Smith's phone rang. He looked worried as he took the call. What was going on?

Will looked at the team again, and saw what the problem was. There were only ten players!

Just then, Steve came running over.

"Smithy has just had a call," he told Will. "Lee's got the flu and can't play! Kingham will be here soon and Smithy thinks we're going to forfeit the match, but I said you'd step in."

At last, thought Will. *I have a chance to prove myself!*

Lee played in midfield, so Will would even be playing in the position he liked best.

"But I haven't got any kit!" he said.

"That's OK," said Steve. "The team kit bag is in the changing room, and there's a pair of boots in lost property."

"I just hope they fit!" said Will, as he rushed off.

Minutes later he was ready.

He jogged out to join the rest of the team. The Ravens shirt was massive on him, and the boots were a size too big, but Will didn't care. He was finally getting a chance to play for the Ravens!

"OK," said Mr Smith. "We are missing a lot of first choice players, but we can still get a result."

He looked at all the players in turn. "The game plan doesn't change; we get the ball forward fast and often, and keep Kingham on the back foot. Stick to your opponents if we lose the ball, and pressure them into making mistakes. We can win this!"

Chapter Six

Making Chances

The ref blew his whistle, and Ravenshill kicked off. Adam passed back to Will from the centre circle, and Will had time to pick a neat pass out before any Kingham players got near him.

A good start, but soon the Ravens were playing their usual style of booting the ball from defence up towards the strikers. This meant the ball came nowhere near Will. But when Kingham got the ball they played a patient passing game.

The Ravens' efforts to closely mark their opponents weren't working – whenever they got near to the ball it was simply passed away.

Steve was getting dragged all over the pitch trying to mark the Kingham left winger. He tracked him into the centre of the pitch – but he'd left a huge gap in defence. Kingham saw it, and were onto it at once.

The left-back surged into the open space, before knocking a simple ball across the box to where their striker was waiting to smash the ball home.

Kingham cheered, and the Ravens players all started shouting at each other, with Steve taking most of the stick.

"What were you thinking, Steve, leaving that gap?" yelled Adam.

"I had to track him, nobody else was there. Why didn't David get back to help?" said Steve.

"He was chasing one of your rubbish passes. Try getting the ball to one of *our* players," said Tom.

"But with you all so far up the pitch, all I can do is hoof it and hope for the best," said Steve. "Maybe if the midfield dropped back we could keep the ball for more than ten seconds."

"Oh, so you know better than Smithy, do you? You're only on the team because everyone is ill!" shouted Tom

Will knew he should speak up for his friend – after all, Steve was only saying the sort of things Will usually said on the touchline – but he wanted to keep out of trouble. So he kept quiet and took his place for kick off.

The ref blew his whistle, and both teams fell back into the same pattern. Ravenshill played the ball forward, lost it, then chased while Kingham passed it around. It was tiring the Ravens out.

Will drifted closer and closer to the defence, hoping to get a touch of the ball. While the other Ravens players chased, he held his position, watching and waiting.

Suddenly Kingham tried a long shot towards the goal, but Will managed to block it. He got the ball under control and looked up to see where his team-mates were.

Adam was tightly marked up front, but David was making a break down the right and had plenty of space.

Will knew he only had a second to make the pass before he was tackled.

Will sent a looping pass down to David. It bounced neatly into David's path. He was able to keep up his running pace and still control the ball, before surging on towards the byline.

The full-back headed across to meet him, but David quickly whipped the ball across the six yard box. Adam smashed the ball towards the goal on the volley, but the Kingham keeper got across to make a great save.

Before Ravenshill could take the corner, the ref blew for half time. But the Ravens had proved they could create chances of their own, thanks to Will.

Chapter Seven

New Tactics

"That last move was much better," said Mr Smith as the players huddled together for their team talk. "Keep on like that and we can get back in the game."

Adam spoke up. "It was all from Will's pass, really."

"Yeah, great pass, Will," said David.

Mr Smith turned and looked at Will. "You're right," he said, "it really was good. We need more of that."

"But Will can't play passes like that if we don't get the ball to him," said Steve. "It's like I said before, we need to use our midfield more. Especially with Will on the pitch."

This time the team were ready to listen. "I'll drop into midfield," said Tom, "and even up the numbers. That should give Will more space on the ball."

Mr Smith nodded. "That could work. So, defence, play the ball out to Will when you get it – "

Will shook his head. "No, you can't just focus on me. If you do then Kingham will just mark me closely and we'll be back where we started. We have to work as a team."

Mr Smith gave Will a hard look. He wasn't used to players telling him what to do. But he thought about it for a bit and then said, "OK. You're right. We'll take Kingham on at their own game. Pass and move, use the space, and try to keep hold of the ball. We're only one goal down, we can win this match!"

Chapter Eight

Turning It Around

The team took their places for the second half, and Will hoped that his advice would work out. Kingham hadn't noticed that Tom was dropping deeper, and when a pass went astray, Tom was there to collect it.

Adam was well marked, so instead he passed the ball back to Will. Will noticed Steve coming up on his right, and played a simple pass out to him. "And back, Steve!" he shouted as he moved forward.

Now in plenty of space, Will steadied himself before rolling the ball neatly through the Kingham defence for Adam to run onto. The Ravens striker got to the ball just ahead of the keeper, and drilled his shot into the bottom right corner of the goal.

"Yes!" Adam sprinted away with his arms in the air, before turning to Will. "Great pass," he said. "Keep it up and we'll win this!"

Will was filled with pride, but there was still most of the second half left to play. Kingham would be looking to get their lead back as soon as possible.

For a while neither side took control of the ball. Kingham had worked out that Will was key to Ravens' better play so they started to mark him very closely.

Time was running out when one of Steve's kicks reached Adam with his back to goal. He moved the ball out to David on the wing, but the Kingham full-back was about to tackle him. Will yelled for David to pass the ball, but before Will could pass it on he was brought down by a Kingham player.

The ref blew for a free kick, and Will struggled to his feet. "I'll take it," he said, and nobody argued with him.

At the start of the match nobody had even wanted him on the team, and now here he was, about to make what might be the most important kick of the game.

Chapter Nine

Free Kick

Will took a deep breath to calm himself, before striking the ball right-footed. It looped over the wall of Kingham players, then began to dip and spin, fooling the goalie.

The ball seemed to move in slow motion as it headed for the top corner, but it kept on curling and hit the top of the post, bouncing back into the packed penalty area.

Will lost track of where the ball was in the mad scramble.

Suddenly the ref blew his whistle and Will saw the ball spinning in the back of the Kingham net.

"Steeeeeve!" the Ravens players shouted.

Will couldn't believe it. In all the chaos, Steve had got his foot to the ball and poked it home.

Will rushed over to his friend, and was pulled into the victory huddle.

The ref blew for full time, and Smithy came onto the pitch to praise the team too.

"Really well done, all of you. You've given me plenty to think about before the next game!" he said, smiling.

Will was over the moon. Steve might have scored the winner, but it was Will who had turned the game around for the Ravens, and the whole team knew it.

Adam and David put him onto their shoulders and carried him off the pitch to the cheers of the rest of the team.

A week ago Will had been a nobody, standing on the sidelines, but now he was the Ravens' hero.

Pitch Dark

David wants to be on the school team, like
he was before. But Nick, the current goalie,
has killed off any hope of that. Walking home
one night, David meets a stranger who will
change his life forever. But will David's
football dream turn into a living nightmare?

ISBN 978-1-4081-5573-8
RRP £5.99

Dead Wood

Holly's family move to the old house so
her dad can do his job: bulldozing the ancient
trees to make way for a housing estate. But
there's something haunting the old house.
Something old, and angry, that doesn't want
the trees cut down. Something *alive*...

ISBN 978-1-4081-6335-1
RRP £5.99

Drawing a Veil

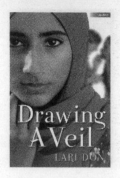

Ellie and Amina are best friends. But when Amina decides to start wearing the hijab, it attracts the attention of the bullies. Does it matter if best friends have different beliefs? A thought-provoking story about friendship, culture and modern life.

ISBN 978-1-4081-5559-2
RRP £5.99

Death Match

While the Nazis occupied Ukraine,
Dynamo Kiev's footballers played matches as
FC Start. Start won, again, and again. Until
they faced a German army side, under the
threat of death if they didn't let the occupiers
win...

ISBN 978-1-4081-4263-9
RRP £5.99

Run, Jimmy, Run

Jimmy can't stand Dax's bullying any longer. He steals £150 from his father and runs away. But Dax is on the same train – and he sees the money. Now Jimmy and Dax are locked in a frantic chase. Can Jimmy run fast enough and far enough?

ISBN 978-1-4081-4259-2
RRP £5.99